Take Care of Our Earth

Written by Gare Thompson

STECK-VAUGHN
COMPANY

A Division of Harcourt Brace & Company

www.steck-vaughn.com

84140

Contents

We Can Help

The Earth gives us many things that we need to live. There are lakes and rivers that give us water to drink. There is wind to bring us fresh air and to cool us on hot days. There is land that gives us food. We need all these things to have good lives.

What happens if the water, air, and land become dirty? That is **pollution**. Pollution is bad for plants, animals, and people.

If water is polluted, we cannot drink it. If air is polluted, it is hard for us to breathe. If the land has too much trash, we cannot find clean places to live and to grow food.

There are things we can do to keep Earth clean and less polluted. We can clean up the places near our homes. We can pick up trash that we see in parks, in school yards, or on sidewalks. We can **recycle** our trash. Everyone should take care of our water, air, and land.

Pollution like this harms the Earth.

Learn About Water

Water is a very important **natural resource** that we get from the Earth. The water you get at home comes from rivers, lakes, and wells. Many water pipes run from a water source such as a lake. Then the water pipes are joined together underground. They bring the water into your home.

When the water reaches your home, all you have to do is turn it on. We use this water to drink, to bathe, and to clean our clothes and dishes. We use it to water our lawns and wash our cars.

Plants need clean water to grow.

Water is very important to farmers. They use water to feed farm animals and to make their crops grow. They need clean rivers and lakes to have safe water.

Rainwater helps to keep crops from drying up. When it is very hot and dry for a long time, there is not enough rain for crops to grow. Then farmers dig many rows of small ditches to move water from the lakes and rivers to their crops. This is called **irrigation**.

Sometimes farmers use irrigation rigs to water their crops.

9

Sometimes the Earth's water gets polluted. Do you know how that can happen? Often factories are built along rivers. Sometimes they dump oil or **chemicals** into the rivers. Then the water becomes polluted. Today there are laws to stop this dumping. Still, some rivers became polluted before the new laws were in place.

Many people, including groups of children, have worked together to clean up rivers and beaches. They have worked hard to make sure that fish have clean water to live in. People enjoy clean rivers, too. They can swim and fish in clean rivers.

Children work to clean up pollution.

Sometimes there is not much rainfall. Rivers and lakes can get low then. Some places have little underground water. So people need to use water wisely to save as much as they can. There are many ways to **conserve** water.

Think of some ways we can use less water. We can be careful to turn off faucets or hoses right after using water. We can water lawns less often. We can take quicker showers.

Use as little water as you can.

A Water Experiment

Is some water polluted? Find out for yourself. You will need:
- three clear jars
- bottled water
- tap water
- pond or lake water

1. Pour one cup of bottled water into a jar.
2. Pour one cup of tap water into another jar.
3. Pour one cup of water from a pond or lake into the third jar.
4. Label the jars and wait one day.
5. Compare the jars the next day.

The bottled water should still look clear. The tap water may look almost as clear. The pond water may look a little dirty. Why? It probably has some pollution in it.

Which of these jars of water would you want to drink?

Learn About Air

Air is everywhere! We cannot see it, but we can often feel it. We can feel the wind. Sometimes the air smells fresh and sweet. At other times, the air may smell dirty and polluted. Polluted air hurts plants and people. Plants don't grow well in polluted air.

People may find it hard to breathe, or they may get sick from polluted air. You may be able to tell if the air is very polluted. Your eyes may burn. Or you may be able to see dirt or smoke in the sky.

Clean air helps people stay healthy.

Cars and trucks pollute the air. Some of their fumes go into the air. Have you ever seen a car that is puffing out smoke? It is making the air dirty. New laws say that all cars have to be fixed so they don't pollute the air.

Many years ago, companies did not know how to protect the air from being polluted. Some factories burned wastes that sent harmful **fumes** into the air. The sky filled with dark clouds of dirt and smoke. This is called **smog**.

Some factories used to pollute the air.

Why is smog so bad? Sometimes smog can hurt your lungs. When you breathe in this dirty air, you fill your lungs with smog. It can make you cough or sneeze.

Many people have learned about smog and have helped clean up the air. They have helped pass laws to make companies stop polluting the air. Today, many companies work hard to keep the air clean. They have found many ways to recycle wastes instead of burning them.

Smog makes some people sneeze or cough.

An Air Experiment

Is the air outside your school dirty? Find out for yourself. You will need:
- two jar lids
- petroleum jelly

1. Put some petroleum jelly on the inside of each jar lid.
2. Place one jar lid on a window sill outside the school.
3. Place the other jar lid on a table in the room. Wait four hours.
4. Compare the two lids. Which lid is cleaner?

You may find some dirt and dust on the inside of the jar lids. The lid that was outside may have more dirt than the other lid. Why? There is probably some pollution in the air outside.

Air can be dirty even when we can't see it.

Learn About Land

We need good land and clean soil for homes and farms. Land can become polluted, too. It can become filled with trash or chemicals. There is pollution when people use harmful chemicals. There is pollution when people throw away too much trash. Then it is dumped into the ground. What can we do?

We can take care of lawns and farms without using any harmful chemicals. We can also recycle most things instead of throwing them away. We can recycle paper, glass, and plastic. This will help to take care of the land.

Recycle to help take care of the land.

A Land Experiment

What happens when different kinds of trash are dumped into the ground? Find out for yourself. You will need:

- three milk cartons
- some wet soil
- a tissue
- a paper cup
- a foam cup

1. Put some soil in each milk carton.
2. Place the tissue in one carton, a piece of the foam cup in another, and a piece of the paper cup in the last carton.
3. Then fill each carton with wet soil.
4. After one week, empty the cartons.
5. Compare the three kinds of trash.

This is what happens when trash is dumped on the land. Some kinds of trash take a long time to break down.

Some kinds of trash take longer than others to break down.

27

Help Save the Earth

Children can help to save the Earth's resources. One way is to plant trees. There is a special day each year called Arbor Day. Children around the world help to raise money to buy trees. Then

Plant a tree to take care of our Earth.

the children plant a tree in the name of someone special.

Some people give trees to others as gifts. The people of Japan gave the United States some cherry trees. The trees were planted in Washington, D.C. Today, these trees add much beauty to the whole city.

Children can help take care of our Earth.

There are many things you can do to take care of the Earth. Here are some groups that work to help take care of the Earth. You may want to write to them for more ideas about how you can help.

Conservation Foundation
1250 24th Street N.W.
Washington, D.C. 20037

Friends of the Earth
1025 Vermont Avenue, N.W.,
Suite 300
Washington, D.C. 20005
www.essential.org

Sierra Club
730 Polk Street
San Francisco, CA 04109
www.sierraclub.org

Glossary

chemicals   things such as acids and gases that
   other things are made up of

conserve   to use less of something

experiment   a test done to prove something

fumes   strong smells

irrigation   using ditches to bring water to
   dry soil

natural resource   something people use that
   comes from the Earth

pollution   harmful things added to the air,
   water, or soil

recycle   to use again

smog   dirty air that has smoke and waste